JASON STRANGE

Cover Art by Alberto Dal Lago

Interior Illustration by Phil Parks

STONE ARCH BOOKS
a capstone imprint

Jason Strange is published by
Stone Arch Books
A Capstone Imprint
151 Good Counsel Drive, P.O. Box 669
Mankato, Minnesota 56002
www.capstonepub.com

Library of Congress Cataloging-in-Publication Data is available at the Library of
Congress website.

Summary: When Lew, Gary and Lugnut are trapped in their middle school basement,
they discover that at night it becomes the domain of zombie teachers and students--will
they survive or be forced to join the undead?

978-1-4342-3234-2 (library binding)
978-1-4342-3433-9 (pbk.)

Art Director/Graphic Designer: Kay Fraser
Production Specialist: Michelle Biedscheid

Photo credits:
Shutterstock: Nikita Rogul (handcuffs, p. 2); Stephen Mulcahey (police badge, p. 2);
B&T Media Group (blank badge, p. 2); Picsfive (coffee stain, pp. 2, 5, 12, 17, 24, 30,
42, 48, 57); Andy Dean Photography (paper, pen, coffee, pp. 2, 66); osov (blank notes,
p. 1); Thomas M Perkins (folder with blank paper, pp. 66, 67); M.E. Mulder (black
electrical tape, pp. 5, 10, 20, 25, 31, 37, 44, 47, 53, 58, 69, 70, 71)

Printed in the United States of America in Stevens Point, Wisconsin.
032011
006111WZF11

TABLE OF CONTENTS

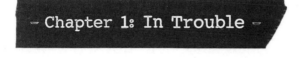

Principal Drone sat on the corner of his desk. His arms were crossed. In front of the principal was Lew Reynolds, that afternoon's first guest.

Principal Drone always called the kids who got sent to his office his "guests." It was supposed to make kids at Ravens Pass Middle School feel safe. It didn't work.

"Do you know why you were sent here, Lew?" Principal Drone asked.

Lew nodded. "Yes," he said. "Because Mr. Finch thinks I wrote my initials on the door to your office. In marker."

Principal Drone smiled. "That's right," he said. "Are you sorry for that?"

"No," Lew said. "I'm not sorry, because it wasn't me."

The principal raised his eyebrows. "Lew," he said, sighing, "the marker said 'L. A. R.' Those are your initials, right?"

"Yes," Lew said. "Lew Andrew Reynolds. But I didn't do it."

"You are the only student in the school with those initials," the principal said. He walked over to the window behind his desk. As he looked out over the playground, he added, "Who else could have done it?"

"Roth," Lew said. "Mort Roth."

"Mort?" Principal Drone repeated. "His initials are not L. A. R., Lew. Why would he write that? If it was him, the initials would have said, 'M. A. R.'"

"I doubt it," Lew said. "I know his real name is Mort Anthony Roth, but everyone calls him Lugnut. He even calls himself Lugnut. Only you and some of the other teachers call him Mort. He hates that name."

The principal stared at Lew for a few minutes. Lew shifted in his seat. "It's true," he said. "Ask anyone."

"What you're saying makes a lot of sense," the principal said. "Okay. Go and get him."

Lew leaned forward. His eyes shot open wide. "Me?" he said. "You want me to go get Lugnut for you?"

"Is that a problem?" the principal asked.

"Yes!" Lew said. "He's probably somewhere he's not supposed to be, for one thing."

"Like where?" Principal Drone said.

Lew shrugged. "The basement?" he suggested. "Down at the pizza place? Hanging out by the railroad tracks? He could be anywhere."

"Hm," the principal said. "I knew Mort was bad news, but I had no idea he got into that much trouble."

"He does," Lew said. He nodded. "He really does. He'll probably beat me up just for talking to him."

"I'm sure you're exaggerating," the principal said. "But, if it makes you feel safer, you can bring a friend."

"What?!" Lew asked, shocked. "You still want me to get him?"

"Just look in the basement," the principal said. He grabbed a pad from his desk and scribbled on it. "Here's a note, so you won't have any trouble getting down there. If anyone asks, just tell them to come and talk to me about it."

"Thanks," Lew said quietly. He took the note.

"No problem," the principal said. He glanced at the clock. "And if you don't find him in the basement, let me know. I don't want you leaving school grounds to find him."

Lew headed for the door.

As Lew left, the principal added, "Please hurry. Last bell is in just a few minutes."

Chapter 2: Into the Basement

A few minutes later, Lew and his friend Gary stood in front of a heavy metal door.

"You have to come with me," Lew said. He had Gary by the wrist. "Safety in numbers."

"No way," Gary said. He pulled his arm away. "I'm not going down there. It's dangerous."

He pointed at the basement door. Signs on the door read "Shock Danger," "No Entry," and "Keep Door Locked."

"Oh, come on," Lew said. "There's no way you can get a shock from just going downstairs."

"That's not why I'm worried," Gary said.

Lew had no answer to that. He wasn't looking forward to meeting up with Lugnut and his friends down there either.

"He's probably not even down there," Lew said. "It's almost three. I bet he left campus hours ago. He's probably down at the tracks by now."

"Or the quarry," Gary said. "My little brother said he saw Lugnut and a few other guys down at the quarry the other day. They were catching frogs and making them fight each other."

"What?" Lew asked, frowning. "Is that even possible?"

Gary shrugged. "I guess so," he said.

"Let's just get this over with," Lew said, shaking his head. He pulled open the door. It opened right away. "I guess they don't really keep it locked."

After climbing down the loud, metal steps, the boys reached a central basement hallway. It was much cooler than the rest of the school. It felt damp, too, and wasn't well lit at all.

The boys walked down the hallway, checking out their surroundings. Pipes and gauges of all shapes and sizes lined the ceiling.

In a few places, smaller hallways branched off the main hall. Some of them were too small for a person to walk down. Lew saw a rat scurry into one of them.

"Ugh," Gary said. "Are those special hallways just for vermin?"

"Who knows," Lew said. He stopped. "Listen."

When the boys were quiet, they heard music echoing down the hall toward them.

"Sounds like heavy metal," Gary said.

Lew nodded. "It's probably Lugnut and his friends," he said. "Come on."

The boys continued on. The music got louder. Soon they started to hear nasty-sounding laughs, then voices.

"It's Lugnut, all right," Lew said. "I'd recognize that evil laugh anywhere."

The hall turned and curved. Finally, Lew and Gary found themselves in a big room. It was full of tanks and pipes and gauges.

The floor was damp and puddles shone here and there. In the center of the room, next to the largest tank, was a group of eighth-grade boys.

One of them wore a baseball cap low over his eyes. He was shaking his fist. Suddenly he tossed a pair of dice onto the floor.

Next to him was a short red-haired boy. He laughed when he looked at the dice. "You lost," he said.

The boy in the cap made an angry face and handed the dice to the third boy. He was the biggest of the three. His T-shirt strained from his huge muscles, and he seemed to have an angry look on his face.

"Lugnut," Lew whispered.

The three boys looked up. Lew swallowed. "Um, hi," Lew said.

"What do we have here?" Lugnut asked. He handed the dice to the red-haired boy and stood up. Then he walked over to Lew and Gary. "What are you dorks doing down here?" Lugnut asked.

The other two boys got up too and hurried over. They stood behind Lugnut. "We should probably teach them a lesson," the boy in the cap said.

"Yeah," the red-haired boy said. "Don't you two dorks know students aren't allowed in the basement?"

Lugnut and his friends thought that was hilarious. All three started hooting and laughing.

"Actually," Lew said, "we were sent here by Principal Drone." He took out the note and held it up.

Lugnut glanced at it and then pushed it away. He wasn't impressed. The other two boys went pale, though.

"You two are working for Drone?" the boy in the cap asked. "Um, I just remembered I have someplace to be."

"Oh, me too," the red-haired boy said. "Let's go."

The two of them scampered off down the hall. Lew and Gary were left alone with Lugnut.

"Those two are afraid of Drone," Lugnut said. "But I'm not. So what do you dorks want down here? Do I have to teach you a lesson about showing up where you're not wanted?"

"Um, no," Lew said. "The principal made us come down here to find you."

"Not us," Gary said. "Just him. Just Lew. I am not working for the principal. I swear."

Lugnut glanced at Gary, then looked back at Lew.

"Why?" Lugnut asked. "Why did Drone want to know if I was down here?"

"He wants to talk to you about your initials on his door," Lew said.

Lugnut smiled. "I wondered when he'd come to me about that," he said. "So why you? Why didn't Drone send the assistant principal or one of the hall monitors?"

"Because first he thought I did it," Lew said. "You and I have the same initials."

"I see," Lugnut said. He stepped closer to Lew. "And you corrected him, huh? Explained that my name is Lugnut, not Mort. Is that right?"

"Yes," Lew said.

"So," Lugnut said. He made two fists and his knuckles popped. Then he went on, "What you're saying is that you ratted me out?"

– Chapter 3: No Escape –

"Run!" Lew said. He didn't need to bother, though. Gary had already taken off down the hall the instant Lugnut cracked his knuckles.

Lew caught up to Gary around the corner. "Thanks for waiting for me," he said between breaths.

"Sorry," Gary said. "My mind was working wrong, because of the fear."

"Mine too," Lew said.

The boys' feet slapped the cement floors as they ran. Their loud breathing echoed through the halls. Behind them, Lugnut started running faster. His feet were heavier and louder.

"You have nowhere to hide," Lugnut shouted.

But the two boys were fast, way faster than Lugnut. They took every turn they could find, hoping to confuse Lugnut.

After running for a few minutes, they couldn't hear his footsteps anymore.

"I think . . . ," Lew said, gasping. "I think we lost him."

They stopped to listen. No footsteps were coming toward them.

Gary leaned over and put his hands on his knees to catch his breath. He nodded.

"Yup," Gary said. "Unfortunately," he added, "I think we also lost ourselves. I have no idea where we are."

"I've been keeping track of our turns," Lew said. "I think I can find our way back to the steps."

Just then, a loud clunk echoed through the basement.

"What was that?" Gary asked.

Lew pulled out his phone to check the time. It was 3:30. School was over.

"I have a bad feeling. I think that was the door locking," Lew said. He glanced at his phone again. "And my cell phone doesn't work down here."

"Great," Gary said, shaking his head. "So we're trapped."

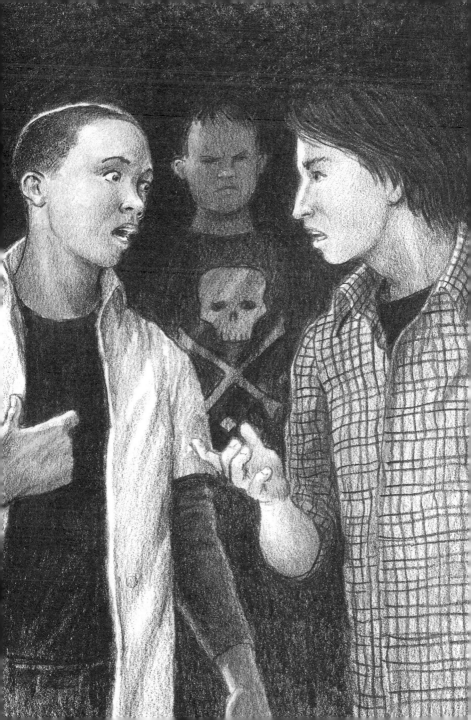

"There must be an emergency exit," Lew said. "Let's look for it."

But as the boys headed back out into the hallway, the lights clicked off. The basement fell into total darkness.

"Uh-oh," Gary said.

Lew and Gary stood still. "Our eyes will get used to it," Lew said. "Don't freak out."

A hand clamped on each of their shoulders and they jumped. "Yeah," a rough voice said. It was Lugnut. "Don't freak out."

The boys pulled away and fumbled around in the dark. They both ended up knocking their heads on the low ceiling of the little hallway.

"I'm sure we can find something to do down here," Lugnut said. Then he laughed.

– Chapter 4: More Trouble –

Lew struggled to pull his collar away from Lugnut, but the bully's grip was too strong.

"Hey," Gary said. "What's that?"

Lew's eyes were adjusting. He could just make out his friend as he pointed into the darkness over Lugnut's shoulder.

"Do I look stupid to you?" Lugnut asked, rolling his eyes. "Do you really think I'd fall for that?"

But it wasn't a trick. Lew saw it too.

A flickering light was coming from around the nearest corner. It was getting brighter.

"No, he's serious," Lew said. "Someone's coming."

Lugnut turned, still holding the boys' collars. He watched the flickering light for a minute, then shook the boys once.

"Listen," he said quietly, "it's probably one of my idiot friends. They probably didn't make it out in time, so now they're looking for me."

He smiled. "I'm going to give them a little scare," Lugnut said. "You dorks stay right here. I'm going to hide by the corner and jump out at them. Don't make a sound. Got it, dorks?"

Lew and Gary nodded.

"Good," Lugnut said. "And like I said, don't move an inch."

He let go of their collars and walked over to the corner. He gave Lew and Gary a cold look and put his finger to his lips to mean *Shh*. Then he slowly ran his finger across his throat.

Lew gulped and nodded.

The light around the corner got brighter. Gary and Lew watched, afraid to move. Lugnut squatted, ready to pounce.

Soon they heard slow footsteps. They were quiet, and it sounded like the person coming had a limp. One of the feet seemed to drag.

Lew could barely see Lugnut's face. But for an instant, the bully seemed afraid.

The light around the corner was very bright. The footsteps were very close. Lugnut cracked his knuckles.

But it wasn't Lugnut's friends.

The flickering light came from an old-fashioned oil lamp. Holding the lamp was a janitor. He held it low, at his waist. When he spotted Lugnut, he stopped short.

"Who's there?" he asked.

Lugnut stood up straight. "Oh, a janitor," he said. "I thought you were someone else. I thought you were —"

But Lugnut stopped talking. Because just then, the janitor raised the lantern to better light up the hallway, and Lugnut saw his face. So did Lew and Gary.

This was no normal janitor.

His skin was holey and peeling off. His hands were black and bony. His clothes were dirty and tattered. His eyes were deep-set and dark, like he didn't have eyes at all.

"What is that thing?" Gary said in a whisper. "It's like the janitor of the undead."

Chapter 5: No Way Out

"No students allowed down here," the undead janitor said. His voice was low and raspy. He spoke slowly, like his tongue might fall out any moment. Lew thought that could happen any time.

Lugnut backed away until he bumped into Lew and Gary. "We have to run," Lugnut said. "It's a zombie."

Gary and Lew nodded. "You've been down here a lot," Lew said. "Lead the way."

Lugnut didn't say anything. He just took off down the hall. Lew and Gary followed, doing their best to keep up.

Lugnut ran at top speed through the basement. He took sharp turns, and he jumped over exposed pipes on the floor. He weaved around tanks and down narrow halls.

"You sure you know where you're going?" Lew asked.

"Positive," Lugnut said. He took a sharp left. "Duck!" he called.

Lew and Gary ducked just in time. They came inches from bonking their heads on a big pipe.

Lugnut took a sharp left turn. "There's the steps," he said, pointing at the door at the top of the stairs. "Told you."

"Oh, good," Lew said.

Lugnut ran up the steps and reached the heavy door. He put a hand on the handle and tugged.

It didn't budge.

"I guess that loud clunk we heard was the door locking," Gary said.

Lew glared at him. "You're not helping," he said. He looked at Lugnut and asked, "Now what?"

"You guys were right before," Lugnut said. He walked back down the steps. "There is an emergency exit, and I know where it is."

Gary crossed his arms. "Why should we trust you?" he asked.

Lugnut shrugged. He started to walk off down the hall.

"What should we do?" Gary asked Lew.

Lew shrugged. "We shouldn't trust him," he said. "But we either go with him or come face to face with the undead custodian."

"Good point," Gary said. The two boys jogged after the bully.

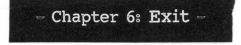

– Chapter 6: Exit –

"It's just through here," Lugnut said. He opened a door. It was only a few feet high, but big enough to squeeze through.

"On the other side of this hall is another boiler room," Lugnut said. The three boys had to crawl to get through. "I used to read comics in there during lunch, back in sixth grade."

At the other end of the tiny hall was another short door. Lugnut pushed it open.

It creaked and squeaked, but finally opened wide enough that they could squeeze through.

Lugnut got out and stood up. For an instant, Lew thought the bully would close the door and lock him and Gary inside the little tunnel. But he just stepped aside and let the two boys climb out.

"Duck as you come in," Lugnut said. "There's a low pipe."

They were in another room like the one they'd found Lugnut and his friends in, only small. There were several big tanks, and pipes running all along the ceiling and the walls.

Across the big room was an emergency exit, like Lugnut had said there would be. It was barely lit by a red exit sign.

In front of the exit was an old library table surrounded by old wooden chairs. They were all half rotted. The table leaned far to one side, where it was missing most of a leg.

But that wasn't the problem. Seated in the chairs were a group of teachers and librarians. Some wore dresses, others ties or jackets. One wore a polo shirt and a whistle around his neck.

And they were all undead.

They hadn't seen the boys come in. They just sat in their chairs. They moaned and drooled. Their skin was normal in some places, but in some places it was gray or green, or it was peeling off like the skin of rotted fruit. One of the teachers — who must have been there longer than the rest — was practically a bare skeleton. Only his bowtie remained.

"Uh-oh," Gary whispered.

Lugnut nodded. "You got that right," he said. "I think we're trapped."

"I thought you come down here all the time," Lew said quietly. "How come you didn't know they were here?"

"Maybe they only come out at night, or something," Lugnut said. "Now be quiet. They haven't seen us yet. Let's head back and stay hidden till we think of a new plan."

Gary and Lew nodded. The three boys headed for the little door. But as he turned around, Gary forgot to duck. He banged his head on a pipe.

"Ow!" Gary shouted. The noise rang out and echoed through the room.

Lugnut and Lew froze. "Maybe they didn't hear," Lew whispered.

The three boys waited. None of them moved an inch. They hoped against hope that no one in the undead faculty meeting had heard them.

But their worst nightmare came true.

"No students allowed down here," a raspy, dry voice said. Chairs scraped on the cement floor as the undead teachers got up. "You'll have to come with us."

"Run!" Lew said. He dove headfirst into the little tunnel. Lugnut and Gary were right behind him.

"Come back here!" a zombie yelled. "No students allowed in the basement!"

"No students allowed in school after dark!" another raspy voice called.

"No students!" groaned another.

"We're almost there," Lew said. He was nearly at the other end of the tiny hall. "Then we can lock the door so they can't get out."

"Good plan," Lugnut said. "Tell your dork friend to close the one on that end too."

"Too late," Gary shouted up the tunnel as he climbed in. "They're right behind me."

Lew climbed out at the other end and looked back down the tunnel. "Hurry!" he shouted.

Lugnut climbed out. Gary was moving too slowly.

"Hurry up, Gary," Lew called out.

"Yes," a raspy voice said at Lew's ear. "Please hurry. We're tired of waiting for you three here."

Lew and Lugnut jumped back. It was the undead janitor. Next to him was someone bigger — bigger even than Lugnut. He was in a black muscle shirt, and he had a tattoo on one shoulder. In fact, he looked a lot like someone Lugnut would hang out with . . . but he was undead.

- Chapter 7: A Bully for the Bully -

The undead bully took Lugnut by the collar. He smiled at him. "Why are you hanging out with these two dweebs?" the zombie asked. "I see you down here all the time, but I've never seen these dorks before."

"Um . . ." Lugnut said.

"I'll tell you what, tough guy," the undead bully said. He pulled out a long rope. "I'll spare you and let you go right now if you help me tie up these dorks."

Lugnut looked at Lew and Gary. "Just tie them up?" Lugnut asked. "That's all?"

"I won't hurt them . . . yet," the undead bully said. "But I might get hungry later. So we can't have them running off, can we?"

The undead bully turned to Lew and Gary as Lugnut watched. The undead bully smiled big. He grabbed Gary by the arm.

"This won't hurt," the undead bully said. Then he smiled and added, "Not much."

Chapter 8: Trapped

"Help us, Lugnut!" Lew shouted. The rope around his arms got tighter as the undead bully pulled the ends.

"Hurry, please," Gary said. "He's going to eat us!"

"He'll kill me too if I try to stop him," Lugnut said. "Sorry, dorks." Then he ran off down the hall.

The undead bully laughed, a deep, slow guffaw. "I knew I liked that guy," he said.

"We have to get out of this on our own," Lew said quietly to Gary. "When I say so, run."

"Run?" Gary whispered back. "How? We're about to be tied up."

The bully bent down to tie together Lew's ankles. As he did, Lew thrust his head forward and slammed it into the bully's head.

The undead bully went sprawling backward. Lew jumped up and pulled off the rope. It was still loose enough that it was easy. Gary got up too.

"Come on!" Lew said. Then the boys ran off after Lugnut.

"I'll get you dorks!" the undead bully yelled. "That headbutt will leave a permanent dent!"

Lew and Gary took off down the hall, but Lugnut was too far ahead. "Which way did he go?" Lew asked.

"What do we want with him?" Gary replied. "He was going to let us get eaten."

"He might know another way out of here," Lew said.

As they ran, Lew struggled to hear signs of Lugnut. He listened for heavy breathing, loud footsteps . . . anything. He finally heard a pop and crackle, then a bang. It sounded like metal hitting metal. Lew wasn't sure what it was, but it was the best clue he had.

"This way," Lew said. He turned down an unfamiliar hallway. Soon they reached a door. "In here," Lew said.

The door was heavy, but together Lew and Gary got it open.

The room was hot. In the middle was a huge incinerator. The room was otherwise mostly empty. A few boxes and bags of garbage were on the floor near the door.

"We have to close the door," Lew said. "Quick." He and Gary leaned on the heavy door, but they were too slow.

The undead bully pushed his way in. "Time for payback," he said, glaring at Lew and Gary. The bully rubbed the dent on his head. Then he cracked his knuckles, just like Lugnut always did.

Gary and Lew were trapped. The bully moved toward them. He was slamming his fist into his palm, ready to pound them into the ground.

The boys backed up. Soon, they were standing right next to the incinerator.

Lew felt his back press up against it, just for an instant. "Ow!" he said. It was burning hot. The fire inside it was raging.

The undead bully laughed. He was getting closer. He reached out for them.

Just then, Lugnut appeared in the open doorway.

"Lugnut!" Lew called out. "Help us!"

The undead bully glanced over his shoulder at Lugnut. Lugnut seemed to be thinking it over. Lew knew he was trying to decide what to do. Should he help the boys? Or should he save his own neck?

The undead bully smiled. Then he dove for Lew.

— Chapter 9: One Down —

"Jump!" Lew shouted. Gary jumped out of the way, and at the very last second, Lew pulled open the iron incinerator door.

"No!" the undead bully cried as he flew headfirst into the incinerator. Lew slammed the door closed.

Gary got to his feet and went to his friend. "Good thinking," he said.

Lew nodded. The two boys looked at Lugnut.

"I was going to help," Lugnut said. "I was working on a plan."

"Sure you were," Lew said. He looked up and around the room. "Maybe there's an exit in here someplace."

"Behind the incinerator," Lugnut said. "That's why I was heading in here."

"Well, we knew it wasn't to help us," Gary said. He and Lew went around behind the incinerator.

"Not so fast," a mean voice said.

The undead gym teacher and janitor both stepped into the room. The gym teacher grabbed Lugnut's arm.

"You kids aren't allowed down here," the janitor said. "We'll take you to the principal. He'll know what to do with you."

"Drone?" Lugnut asked. "You know him?"

"Who's Drone?" the gym teacher asked. "Down here, we have our own principal." He laughed, and Lew saw his rotting teeth.

Then Gary whispered, "Here's the exit." Lew looked over. Gary had found a grate, and behind it was a duct. It was just wide enough for Lew and Gary to fit through. "Come on!" Gary said.

Lew ran over to Gary and followed him into the vent.

"Wait!" Lugnut said. He tried to pull away, but the zombie was far too strong. His decaying hand wouldn't budge.

"Just a minute, boy," the undead gym teacher said. "Your friends destroyed our bully down here. He'll need to be replaced right away."

The janitor leaned close to Lugnut's face. There was decay and death in the zombie's breath as he said, "I know just the boy for the job."

- Chapter 10: Above Ground -

Lew and Gary climbed out through a heavy grate in the back room of the cafeteria. Through a nearby window, Lew saw the sun had already gone down.

"I guess the spooks come out at night," Gary said.

Lew nodded. "I hope they stay in the basement," he said. He pulled out his phone. "Now let's get out of here."

Before long, the police were there, and then Lew's parents and Gary's parents. Everyone gathered on the big lawn just outside the cafeteria. The night air was warm and smelled fresh and safe.

Principal Drone showed up before long and walked right up to Lew.

"So?" the principal said. "Did you find Lugnut?"

"Yes," Lew said. "But he . . . I don't think he made it out of the basement."

"He's still down there?" Principal Drone asked. He grabbed the arm of a policeman who was walking by. "Haven't you searched the basement yet, officer?" Principal Drone asked.

"Of course," the officer said. "There was another boy down there. He's right there."

He pointed down the lawn, where Lugnut was talking to an older man. Lew thought it was probably Lugnut's dad.

The guy seemed pretty angry. Lugnut looked like he was in big trouble.

"How did he get away?" Gary whispered to Lew. "Those two zombies were right behind him."

Lew shrugged. "Come on," he said. "Let's go ask."

The two boys walked toward Lugnut and his father. As they got closer, his father stopped shouting and stormed off.

Lugnut looked up as Lew and Gary walked over.

"We're glad you're okay," Lew said.

"I'm not," Gary said.

"Um, whatever," Lugnut mumbled. He scratched his ear and a big piece of his earlobe fell off. He quickly bent over, picked it up, and tried to stick it back on.

Lew and Gary looked at him, wide-eyed. "You're . . . you're . . . ," Lew stammered.

"Decaying," Lugnut said. He shrugged. "So they got me, and I'm one of them. That doesn't mean I have to stay in the stupid school basement all the time."

Lew and Gary started to back away, but Lugnut grabbed their collars. "If you guys tell anyone about this," the undead bully said, "I'll eat your brains." Then he ran away, into town.

Case number: 4452133

Date reported: April 10

Crime scene: Ravens Pass Middle School, Ravens Pass

Local police: Officer Bob Randall, with the force 15 years

Victims: Lew Reynolds, age 15; Mort "Lugnut" Roth, age 16 (whereabouts unknown); Gary Wilson, age 15

Civilian witnesses: Faculty and students at Ravens Pass Middle School; parents of missing students

Disturbance: Three students were reported missing after entering the Ravens Pass Middle School basement. Upon questioning, I determined the actual disturbance to be an infestation of undead.

Suspect information: Undead hive "living" in the school basement.

CASE NOTES:

WHEN POLICE QUESTIONING WASN'T GETTING ANYWHERE
WITH THE TWO VICTIMS WHO REMAINED ON THE SCENE,
THEY CALLED ME IN.

RIGHT AWAY, I KNEW SOMETHING WAS UP. EVENTUALLY
THE BOYS CONFESSED THAT "LUGNUT" HAD FLED THE
SCENE, AND FROM THE WAY THEY GOT NERVOUS, I
KNEW IT WOULDN'T BE GOOD WHEN WE FOUND HIM.
THEY WOULDN'T TELL ME EXACTLY WHAT THEY'D SEEN
IN THE BASEMENT, BUT A SIMPLE SEARCH WAS ENOUGH
TO TELL THE TRUE TALE.

I ORDERED SCHOOL OFFICIALS TO SEAL THE BASEMENT
DOORS WITH STEEL, AND AS SOON AS SCHOOL'S OUT,
WE'LL BEGIN THE EXTERMINATION. IN THE MEANTIME,
REMAINING MEMBERS OF THE HIVE WON'T HURT
ANYONE.

AS FOR LUGNUT—HE'S STILL AT LARGE. BUT I'LL FIND
HIM. I HAVE NO DOUBT ABOUT THAT.

DEAR READER,

THEY ASKED ME TO WRITE ABOUT MYSELF. THE FIRST
THING YOU NEED TO KNOW IS THAT JASON STRANGE IS
NOT MY REAL NAME. IT'S A NAME I'VE TAKEN TO HIDE MY
TRUE IDENTITY AND PROTECT THE PEOPLE I CARE ABOUT.
YOU WOULDN'T BELIEVE THE THINGS I'VE SEEN, WHAT I'VE
WITNESSED. IF PEOPLE KNEW I WAS TELLING THESE STORIES,
SHARING THEM WITH THE WORLD, THEY'D TRY TO GET ME TO
STOP. BUT THESE STORIES NEED TO BE TOLD, AND I'M THE
ONLY ONE WHO CAN TELL THEM.

I CAN'T TELL YOU MANY DETAILS ABOUT MY LIFE. I CAN TELL
YOU I WAS BORN IN A SMALL TOWN AND LIVE IN ONE STILL. I
CAN TELL YOU I WAS A POLICE DETECTIVE HERE FOR TWENTY-
FIVE YEARS BEFORE I RETIRED. I CAN TELL YOU I'M STILL
OUT THERE EVERY DAY AND THAT CRAZY THINGS ARE STILL
HAPPENING.

I'LL LEAVE YOU WITH ONE QUESTION—IS ANY OF THIS TRUE?

JASON STRANGE
RAVENS PASS

Glossary

custodian (kuhss-TOH-dee-uhn)—someone whose job is to clean a large building

decay (di-KAY)—rotting

exaggerating (eg-ZAJ-ur-ate-ing)—making something seem bigger, better, more important than it is

flickering (FLIK-ur-ing)—flashing on and off

gauges (GAYJ-iz)—instruments for measuring something

grounds (GROUNDZ)—the area around a building

incinerator (in-SIN-uh-ray-tur)—a furnace for burning garbage and other materials

permanent (PUR-muh-nuhnt)—lasting or meant to last for a long time

surroundings (suh-ROUN-dingz)—the things or conditions around someone

undead (uhn-DED)—someone who is technically dead but can still move

unfamiliar (uhn-fuh-MIL-yur)—not known

vermin (VUR-min)—small, common insects or animals that are harmful pests

DISCUSSION QUESTIONS

1. What are some good ways to handle bullies?

2. If you could be one of the characters in this book, who would you want to be? Explain your answer.

3. What other creepy things do you think are in the Ravens Pass Middle School basement? Talk about them!

WRITING PROMPTS

1. What if there were a group of undead teachers in your school? Describe them!

2. Imagine this story from Lugnut's point of view. Try writing the last chapter from his perspective.

3. The principal in this book is named Principal Drone. Write about the principal at your school.

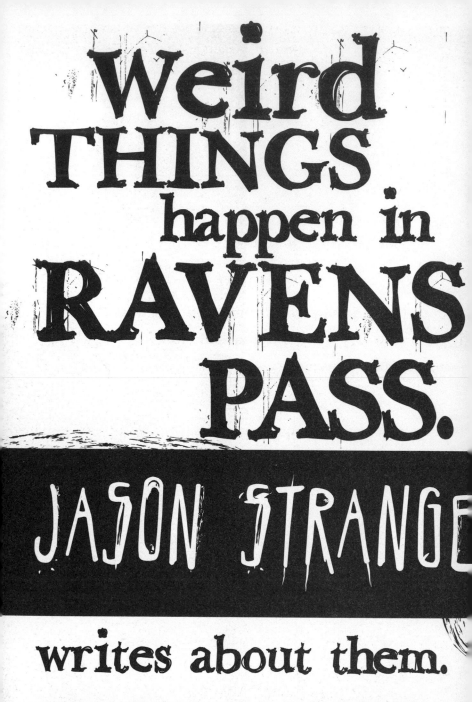